burn

burn

ALMA FULLERTON

DANCING CAT 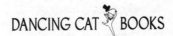 BOOKS

First published in the United States in 2011
Text and illustrations copyright © 2010 Alma Fullerton
This edition copyright © 2010 Dancing Cat Books,
an imprint of Cormorant Books Inc.
This is a first edition.

The publisher gratefully acknowledges the support of the
Canada Council for the Arts and the Ontario Arts Council for its publishing program.
We acknowledge the financial support of the Government of Canada
through the Canada Book Fund for our publishing activities.

 Canada Council Conseil des Arts
for the Arts du Canada

 ONTARIO ARTS COUNCIL
CONSEIL DES ARTS DE L'ONTARIO

Library and Archives Canada Cataloguing in Publication

Fullerton, Alma
Burn / Alma Fullerton.

ISBN 978-1-897151-95-2

I. Title.

PS8611.U45B87 2010   jC813'.6   C2010-904416-9

U.S. Publisher Cataloging-in-Publication Data
(Library of Congress Standards)
United States Library of Congress Control Number: 2010931060
Fullerton, Alma.
Burn / Alma Fullerton.
[255] p. : ill. ; cm.
Summary: Since taking over the care of the house and her autistic sister, Casey has little
time to mourn their mother's desertion. At first she finds comfort sending smoke signals
and imagining that they will find her mom, but soon the small fires aren't enough; and
what starts out as a harmless ritual gets out of control.
ISBN-13: 978-1-897151-95-2 (pbk.)
1. Novels in verse. 2. Abandoned children — Juvenile fiction.
3. Pyromania — Juvenile fiction. 4. Emotional problems — Juvenile fiction.
4. Mothers and daughters — Juvenile fiction. I. Title.
[Fic] dc22   PZ7.5.F8554Bur   2010   LCCN: 16295012

JUV013070 Juvenile Fiction/Family/Siblings
JUV039050 Juvenile Fiction/Social Issues/Emotions & Feelings
JUV039140 Juvenile Fiction/Social Issues/Self-Esteem & Self-Reliance

Cover design: Angel Guerra/Archetype
Cover image and interior illustrations: Alma Fullerton
Interior text design: Tannice Goddard, Soul Oasis Networking

 Mixed Sources
Product group from well-managed forests,
controlled sources and recycled wood or fiber
FSC www.fsc.org Cert no. SW-COC-000952
© 1996 Forest Stewardship Council

Manufactured by Transcontinental Gagné, with 100% post-consumer waste recycled paper
in Louisville, Quebec, Canada in August 2010. Job# 41237.

Dancing Cat Books

An imprint of Cormorant Books Inc.
215 Spadina Avenue, Studio 230, Toronto, Ontario, Canada M5T 2C7
2250 Military Trail, Tonawanda, New York, USA 14150
www.dancingcatbooks.com • www.cormorantbooks.com

Meltdowns

Those daytime talk shows
usually bore me to death,
but Mom gobbles them up
like chocolate.

She's watching IVAN
—one of her favorites—
when Ginny and I walk in from school.

"Come watch this, Casey," Mom says.
"That new singer,
Dani Whatsherface,
is coming on soon."

"Winterburn," I say, dropping
a puzzle on the floor for Ginny
and waiting until she's occupied
before I go to sit with Mom.

It doesn't take long.
Ginny gets right to the puzzle,
piecing it together in squares,
always working from the outside in.
No two pieces out of order.

"Wow, look at that dress,"
Mom says.
"If you call *that* a dress."

Dani dances on stage
wearing a shiny space suit dress-thing
with lit-up pointed metallic boobs.

"She's young
—like what—twenty?" Mom says
almost in a whisper. Her eyes glaze over.
She looks lost.

"Yeah," I say. While Dani's singing,
I watch Mom's expressions change
faster than a rock star
changes clothes midshow.

Both are disguises.
The clothes and the expressions.

"She's good," Mom says.

"Yeah, pretty good."

Ivan stands and claps
as Dani walks to the couch.

"Dani ... Dani ..." He shakes her hand.
"FAB-U-LOUS!"

That's when I mostly tune out.

The interview is the
same old same old.
I'm closing my eyes,
listening for the one thing
I don't want Ivan to say.

Don't ask it, Ivan.
PLEASE don't say it.
Not while she's watching.

"So what does it feel like
to be called the next
Libby McCall?" Ivan says.

"Crap," I whisper.

"Is that what they're calling HER?"
Mom says. She snaps off the TV
before we hear Dani's answer
and chucks the remote across the floor.

It skids over Ginny's puzzle,
breaking it apart.
Ginny cries.
"It's wrecked!"

But Mom doesn't pay attention.
"They are calling HER
the next LIBBY MCCALL?"
Mom says
over Ginny's screeching.

All I can do is nod.

"HOW can SHE be
the next Libby McCall
when I AM RIGHT HERE?"

I bite my upper lip
and look down.

"You're here, Mom," I whisper,
"but you're not out *there*."

Mom stares at me for a few seconds
before collapsing into a ball on the floor
beside Ginny.

And both of them rock their way

back and forth,

into their own heads,
leaving me standing
in the real world
all alone.

Straight-UP Kid

I shouldn't have said
that last part.
Not out loud.
Not to Mom

I shouldn't have said it.
I was on dangerous ground
and I knew
she'd crack.

But it's the truth,
and I've always,
ALWAYS
been a straight-up
slap-you-in-the-face
-with-truth kind of kid.

Mom taught me to be that way.

If you want to know
how you look in a dress,
ask Mom or me
and we'll tell you.

Nothing but straight up
comes out of our mouths.

Why try searching your brain
for better (more proper?) words
when the best way to say it
is right there?

"That dress makes you look like a cow."

The truth is never disguised.

Le Bistro

I need to get away,
so I head down the street
to John's restaurant.

He gives me a big hug
and swings me around
when I walk in.
"What's going on with
my girl?" he asks.

I love when he calls me
his girl, because
I'm really not his at all,
but he always makes me feel like
I am.

I breathe him in
while he's got me close
—garlic, oregano, and mint—
Mediterranean must be today's special.

"Mom's having a bit of a meltdown," I say.
"She'll be fine. Like always.
But for now, can I stay here?"

"What's Ginny doing?" he asks.

"Melting with her," I say.
"I'll give them an hour
and go back and check on them."

John rubs his hands together.
"A whole hour of free labor.
Come on. You can
help me prep for the dinner crowd."

"Yes!" John knows I love it when
I'm allowed to cook beside him.

When I get home,
Mom has everything
back under control.

She's playing one of her CDs
and she's on the floor with Ginny,
piecing together the puzzle
like nothing happened.

"I brought dinner," I say,
holding up the takeout bag.

Smoke Signals

I'm jolted awake
by the beating of a drum,
and scramble to my window
to check it out.

Smoke-swirls rise from the clearing
in woods behind my house.

Mom ...

I rush through the kitchen
and freeze when I see
it's almost ten o'clock.

Crap, Ms. Watts is going to have a cow.
I'm late again—
and this time it's not like fifteen minutes late,
it's almost two hours.

Why didn't Mom wake me up?

Dew from the grass seeps
between my feet and my flip-flops.
I should have worn sneakers because,

as I continue through the woods,
pine needles and dirt stick to the wet,
and it looks like I'm wearing
black and green prickly slippers.

When I get closer,
the drumming is so loud
it covers up my squishing footsteps.

I pass the last string of trees
and find Mom dancing by a campfire.
She's chanting and beating on a djembe
held in front of her on shoulder straps.

She's wrapped in a gray blanket of smoke.
It flows around her like a long skirt,
breaking up and swirling toward the sky in spirals
every time she raises her hands and spins.

A twig snaps under my foot.

"I've been sending smoke signals,"
she says in midspin.
"A message to the higher powers to
send me a sign."

"A sign about what?" I ask.

"Whatever is next for me
in this train ride called life."

"Does it work?
The smoke signals?"

"Always."

She puts her djembe down
and pulls food from a bag by her feet.
Marshmallows, graham crackers,
two chocolate bars,
and a jar of strawberry jam.
"You hungry?"

"S'mores?
For breakfast?" I ask.

"Why not?" she says.
"Add a dollop of strawberry jam,
wash it down with milk,
and you have three food groups."

"John will have a heart attack
if he finds out," I say.

She rolls her eyes.
"John is too busy at the restaurant
to know what we're doing here.
And what he doesn't know
won't hurt him."

"Why didn't you wake me?" I ask.
"And where's Ginny?"

"I drove her to school,
but I wanted you home.
This is a You-and-Me day, Casey.
Just like when you were little,
and we were on the road.
Those were the best days, weren't they?
Those days of just us?"

I nod, shifting my feet.
My belly sinks at the thought of
the real meaning behind those words.

Mom raises her eyebrows, knowing
she's made me uncomfortable.
"I decided it was about time
we had a You-and-Me day again.
Know what that means?"

"No."

"It means we can do anything
we damn well please."

"The indoor amusement park just opened," I say.

"Why not?"

"YES!"

Whispers from the Past

It still happens
when Mom gets into crowds.

It always starts
with the half-whispers.
"Is that Libby McCall?"

We both turn and smile
at the sound of
her name.

"Ohmigod, it is!
And look! Little Casey is
almost all grown up!"

Suddenly we're signing
autographs on slips of paper,
backpacks, shoes, foreheads, hands,
and in two cases—for Mom anyway—butts.

Six years after her last album
hit the stores
and we're still getting mobbed.

When we reach the front
of our roller-coaster line
and go through the gate, we know
the thrill of the crowd
is way better than the ride will be.

"Libby, when is your next album coming out?"
Someone calls as we're strapped into the seats.

Mom only shrugs.
"Soon."

Sweet.

Why a Caged Bird Sings

"What happened back there, Casey," Mom says
as we turn onto the highway to home,
"all those people still wanting more.
That was the sign I needed.
I have to get back out there."

"They love you, Mom," I say.

"Remember when you were about four
and I did that talk-show stint?" she says.

"Yeah. You sang
'Complicated Love,'" I say.

"That's right. Remember when
Maya Angelou read you the poem
'Caged Bird'?"

"I remember it cradled me like a hug."

"Do you understand it?" she asks.

"I think so," I say.
"I think it means he's singing
for his freedom and hoping
someone hears?"

"Close enough," Mom says.
"But anyway, that's exactly
how I feel here, Casey.
Stuck in this town.

I'm screaming a song
of freedom."

"I totally understand, Mom.
I feel like that too.
We're two peas in a pod—
me and you—right?"

"Two peas in a pod," she whispers.

"Mom, if I find the key to your cage door,
I'll open it for you."

"Promise?"

"Cross my heart."

The Days of Her and Me

I had a valid passport
from the time I was born
until I was almost six.

Mom took me everywhere,
even on stage to sing a song with her.

We jetted concert to concert.
Recording to Recording.
City to City,
Country to country—

just Mom and me.

Mom was always biggest
in Australia and Europe.

Then a couple of songs
on her last CD reached
number one on the US charts.

About the same time,
four other things happened:

1. Grandma Jean died
   and we came here for the funeral,
2. Mom got reacquainted with John
   —an old high-school flame.
3. She got pregnant with Ginny—an oops.
4. And I needed to go to school.

John convinced her to
Settle down.
Get a stable sort of life.
So Mom vanished
from the music business
—for us.

Gone in midair—
according to some,
and to most of those people
Midair would be exactly
where she went.

But now that she's got her sign,
she'll be ready to get back
to the way things were.

Australia better watch out,
because here comes the
McCall-Hills family.

Ginny Being Ginny

Ginny sits at her desk, filing
her pencil crayons back in the box.

"Come on, Ginny," Mom says.
"We want to get home."

"No use trying to force her, Mom.
She needs to finish her routine
or she'll throw a fit," I say.

Ginny's aid Ms. Emm smiles.
"You must be feeling better, Casey."

"I wasn't sick," I say.

Mom gives me a panicked look,
like a child
sneaking a snack before dinner.

"Dentist appointment in Toronto this morning."
I click my teeth together
and grin wide enough to show them.
"Nice choppers, eh? No cavities."

"You go all the way to Toronto
to see a dentist?" Ms. Emm asks.

"Yep, Dr. Wong has been my dentist
since I was real little.
Sometimes I don't like change,
almost as much as Ginny," I tell her.
"And I certainly don't want to get
the WONG dentist mad."

I giggle at my own joke
and so does she.

"The cool thing is we had an hour
to stop at the new indoor amusement park
and go on a couple rides."

"Fun," Ms. Emm says, packing up her papers.
"I'll see you tomorrow, then?"

"Yep. Have a good night."
I watch her leave.

"Smart girl," Mom says.
"Now we don't have to explain
to anyone why we were at the park
if it hits the news." Mom glances at Ginny.
"Are you almost done?"

Ginny pays no attention.
She's stuck on her pencils.
"Blues, purples, reds, oranges ..."
She puts each perfectly sharpened pencil away
in order.

Ginny is all about order.

A blue pencil slides out of the box
and rolls off her desk.
The order is messed up.

She slams the box against the desk
and whips her pencils across the room
one by one.

Mom grabs Ginny's hands to
make her stop,
but Ginny kicks at Mom until
she breaks her down.

Mom gives up
and sinks to the floor,
resting her forehead on her knees
to wait it out.

I scramble to pick up the pencils
and sharpen their broken tips
to perfect points.

When I get back to Ginny,
she's banging her hands
on the desk—sobbing.

"Ginny—Ginny!" I say.
"Look, your pencils are pointed
—let's start again.
Blues, purples, reds, oranges.
Blues, purples, reds, oranges."

Ginny sniffs, hiccups, and wipes her face.
She picks up the blue
and begins again.

When I look at Mom,
she's watching us.
Her expression tells me
another sign is forming
in her brain.

"You can do it," she whispers.

"Do what?" I ask.

"Handle Ginny
if I get back into the business.
You can handle her."

Friday Night Ritual

Norah is sleeping over.
It's been a ritual with us
since we were seven.
Friday night at my house.

We're zipped tight inside our
sleeping bags in the pop-up tent
Mom pitched in the basement.

"Mom's going to Toronto
to cut another CD," I say.

"Really?" Norah says.

"Yep. She said so. Soon.
And we're all going to end up
on the road with her for a while.
Maybe to Australia."

"No kidding?"
Norah's eyes widen.
"What about school?
And Ginny?"

"There's only a couple of months left
until school's done for the summer,
and I can take care of Ginny.
When Mom's on stage.
Mom already told me so."

"Can I come?
If it's just for the summer?" Norah asks.
"If I'm left here, I won't have
anyone to play with."

"You could call Sarah," I say.

"Girly-Girl Sarah?" Norah says. "No thanks.
She whines way too much and, besides,
I'm not into dressing up like dolls
and glopping clown makeup on my face."

"I bet Mom would say a big YES
to you coming for the summer, anyway," I say.
"Besides, if you didn't come,
we'd break our weekend ritual.
Rituals must not be broken.
It's bad luck.

And you know how
my mom is all about rituals."

High fives!

"BFFs Forever!" we say together.

Night Conversations

Norah is fast asleep.
Her heavy breathing mixes with
a whole orchestra of tree frogs
having conversations outside.

One conversation interrupts
all of the others, and this one
I need to listen to closer.

"I have to go back out there, John," Mom says.
"I'm dying here."

"You can go to Toronto to cut a CD
and still be home at night," John says.

"It's not that easy," Mom says.

"Singers do it all the time," John says.

"Unlike other people, we don't live near a studio.
I'd have to be in a studio twelve or more hours a day.
And with a CD comes a tour.
I've been writing songs for six years, John.

Six years of nothing but writing.
I'm losing my mind here."

"What about the girls' lives?
And mine. What about us?"

"You could come.
Summer is almost here," Mom says.

"Ginny can't handle that life.
YOU know that.
And there's the restaurant,
I can't just up and leave. And Casey—"

"Casey can handle anything.
John, I can't stay."

"Then go," John says.

A door slams. Opens again.
They've gone to another room
and I can't hear them anymore.

Mom comes back after a while
and the only noise that fills my ears
is her crying.

Packing

"That's it.
I guess this is how it has to be,"
I say as I stuff clothes
into my old suitcase.
I have to be ready
as soon as Mom gives
the word.

Ginny's sitting on my bed
matching up my socks.

"John is right and Mom knows it.
He can't leave the restaurant,
and you can't leave your routine.
You just can't handle change.
And the road—it's a HUGE change."

I swallow hard but don't cry.
Last night, Mom cried enough
for both of us, and one of us
needs to be strong.

"I'll miss you and John.
You know that, right?

But we'll come back
between shows,
and we'll call all the time."

I suck on my top lip.
No tears.

"It's the way things are—
always have been.
Mom and me,
Two peas in a pod.
We can't live a settled life."

I take the socks away from her
and she screams,
"Give them back!"

"You've matched them all, thanks," I tell her.

"You're welcome. Give them back," she says.

"Can't." I toss them into my suitcase
and zip it up, shoving it into my closet.
"Ready to jet."

"Ready to jet," Ginny repeats.

Snubbed

I wake up late again,
but this time it's not to drumming,
it's to Ginny screaming.

I stand in the kitchen, tapping my foot
as I watch Mom put a bowl of oatmeal
in front of Ginny.

I dance around them,
doing a whacked-out Egyptian dance.
Waiting for Mom to see me.
Waiting for her to say,
"Sorry for not waking you up, Casey."

But she's ignoring me.
Totally.

"Just standing here,
hanging out,
waiting for some love," I say,
still dancing
—this time directly in front of her.

But she's not paying attention.

Then it occurs to me
maybe today is the day
she's going to tell me
we're leaving.
"Do you want me home again?" I ask.

"No, you're going to school," she says.
She's speaking in monotone
and still doesn't glance in my direction.

"Oh." I plunk down at the table to eat.
"Then why didn't you wake me?"

"I did. You just didn't wake up."
She's turned away.

Being ignored is driving me nuts, so
I'm drumming on the table
with my spoon.

No reaction.

Mom wipes down the microwave.

"Don't make plans after school, please.
I need you to look after Ginny.

I have some things to do."
She finally says something to me
without a question first.

"Okeydokey, Mom,
I can handle Ginny until you get back,
no problemo." I'm dancing again—
this time the "Charlie Brown,"
but my insides are flipping nerves,
because Mom still isn't smiling
or even looking at me.

I jump on the counter beside the microwave
to get right in her face.
"So, what you doing later?"

"Stuff." She turns away quickly
and loads the dishwasher.

"Are you freaking mad
at me for something, Mom?
If you are,
I'd like to damn well know
what it is! Because I don't think
I did anything wrong."

Mom spins around
and glares at me.
"I AM NOW!"

"Fine! I'm going then!"
I hop off the counter
and stomp away,
slamming the door as I leave,
without even bothering
to give her a kiss
good-bye.

Telling Norah

I don't tell Norah
about the fight
that went on while she slept.
Or that John told Mom
to *just go*.

All I tell Norah is,
"Mom wants it to be just
me and her. That's the way
she likes it.
And we don't know for sure when
we'll be coming back.
So you can't come."

"I bet you didn't even ask," Norah says.
She stomps off to the choir room.

I watch her leave and don't tell her
she's right, because
Mom was too busy snubbing me
this morning to even let me know
when we're going.

Recess School Choir Practice

Words

       tones

           rhythms

       beats

voices

       music

          rings through me.

       Shivering

its way

     up

       and down

   my arms.

                        sounding

      Soothing breaths   r   just

fill my world   ai   like

       with song   he   Mom's.

         and everyone   t

stops   h

   to listen   ug

   when my voice rises   thr^o

   from my belly

              and fl o a^{ts}

When I sing, the world around me
disappears and I can forget
all of the drama going on
in my life.

Friends Can Be So Mean

"The only reason
Casey gets those solos
is because her mom is famous.
Casey sings
like a dying crow."
Sarah Cunningham's
lies make me crash
to the ground.

They crack me open
like an egg falling
on the floor of John's restaurant.

And Norah should
stand up for me.

Norah should
rip one into her
for being mean to me,
but that doesn't happen.

Norah agrees with her,
because she's still mad at me
and she's sucking up to
that dress-up-doll-Sarah
all because I told her
Mom didn't want her to come.

And for the rest of practice,
I want to scream like Ginny,
because singing doesn't even make me
forget the drama going on.

How can I forget the drama when
its queens are standing
right behind me?

Stand Up for Yourself

Mom always tells me,

boys shouldn't be
picking on girls,
under any circumstances,

but on the way home
Aaron Taylor kicks every girl
coming off the playground.

I go before Ginny.
So I can make sure
she won't get kicked.

When Aaron kicks at me,
I grab his foot and yank.

And as he slips
onto the wet grass,
I kick him

HARD.

"That'll teach you for kicking girls."
I pull Ginny past him
and stomp off the playground,
not worrying about
any trouble I'm going to get in.
Aaron started it
and Mom will stick up for me.

Aaron curls up—shin in hand,
howling.

The boys around laugh at him.
Because he got beat up by a girl.

Their teasing brings a lump
to my throat.
But I push it away.
I'm not going to waste my time
feeling sorry for Aaron.

Instead, I focus on Norah and Sarah,
Their fists pumping in the air
as they cheer,
        "Way to go, Casey!"

I give them my biggest smile
and pump my fist too,
because no matter
how mad I was at them earlier,

a rotten boy will always make
fighting girls
become friends again.

The Envelopes

When Ginny and I get home,
there are two envelopes on the table.

Addressed in Mom's handwriting.

One for John.
One for me.

I turn mine over
but don't open it.

I can't open it.

Envelopes don't mean

I'll be back for dinner

and they don't mean

See you later

but *See you next time I'm in town.*

Envelopes mean
a LOT longer than just
after school.

It's All My Fault

Don't come near me stay out of my way I'm going
to slam doors punch someone throw something
kick out a window smash a hole through the wall
rip apart my room knock over furniture break
everything in the kitchen I'm going to   SCREAM
                SCREAM
                        S C R E A M
                                my freaking head off

I should have just kept
my mouth shut.

But I had to be honest,

straight up with
You're here, Mom,
but you're not out there.

And she just had to
pick this time to listen.

Blaming Someone Else

I throw my envelope back on the table
and pick up John's.
I race to the restaurant,
dragging Ginny behind me
the whole way.

By the time we get there,
Ginny's screaming her head off
from all my tugging
and John's customers
are staring.

I give them my best google-eyed
none-of-your-flippin'-business look
until they turn away.

"Casey?" Lulu, John's assistant manager, says.
"What's going on?"

I storm past her
and into the kitchen,
because Lulu is not the person
I need to yell at.

"She's gone," I say,
slamming his letter
against the butcher block
he's cutting on.

John looks at me, stunned,
and then down at the letter.

"Oh."

"That's all you can say?
OH?" I yell at him.

"Casey, my girl, I—"

"DON'T CALL ME THAT.
I'm not YOUR GIRL!
My mother is gone
and it's ALL YOUR FAULT!
YOU told her to leave
—without us!
MOM is not a settler,
and neither am I."

I shove him against his butcher block
and run out of the restaurant,
not caring who or what
I knock over along the way.

Running

I can outrun
almost any boy in my class
but I will

never

be able to outrun
what I know.

Mom and I are exactly the same.
If she couldn't last here,
how will I?

It knocks me down
and winds me.

Rain

John finds me
on a bench
overlooking the bay.

"Temperature is dropping fast," he says.
"It's supposed to snow this weekend."

"It'll be a cold
Mother's Day," I say
with a sarcastic edge.
"Big difference from
the summer weather of
last weekend, isn't it?"

John sits on the bench
and wraps his arm
around my shoulder.

The wind picks up. It blasts
our faces with icy thorns as
we stare silently
over the never-ending gray
where the sky meets water.

Smoke Signals

Out in the clearing
the air is cold and still.

I don't know how to send
smoke signals through the air
like Mom does.

But if I burn a piece of paper
and let the smoke roll up to
hold my hand
where hers would hold it,
close my eyes,
and whisper a wish,

Please don't leave me

then let go,
will my words
float through the sky
on the wings of gray swirls
to reach her?

Mom said,

"Always."

She'll Come Back

I don't know what
I was worried about.

Mom would never
leave me
—not for long.

But that envelope is still
staring at me from the table
when I get home.

I pick it up and
throw it to the back of my desk,
hiding it and the words inside.

No need to read the letter now.
Mom will see the smoke signal
and come back.

Then, if she wants,
we can pull out that letter
and turn it into a song later.

To us—everything
is a song.

Piano Lessons

"It's six o'clock," Ginny says.
"Where's Mom?"

"Mom is not here.
She's recording in Toronto.
She'll be back in a few days—tops."

"It's six o'clock!" Ginny says.
"Time for the piano."

"Mom is not here!" I say.

"SIX O'CLOCK. SIX O'CLOCK
PIANO LESSONS!" Ginny says.

"Ginny, Mom is not home,
and I don't play the piano."

"SIX O'CLOCK."

"Ginny, things change.
There is no lesson today."

Ginny runs to the piano
and bangs on the keys.
"IT'S SIX O'CLOCK!
SIX O'CLOCK!"

"Ginny, you don't have to have
a major meltdown
over some STUPID piano lessons!"
I yank her away from the piano
and slam down the lid.
"Mom is NOT here.
DEAL WITH IT!"

Ginny sinks to the floor. "Piano lessons."

She's not dealing.

I suck on my upper lip,
watching her
"Can you practice your scales?
I'll play along on my guitar."

"Piano," Ginny whimpers.

I open the lid on the piano for her,
pick up my guitar,
and play chords.

Ginny sits at the piano
and plays along.

Maybe I *can* help Ginny deal,

because when it comes to
stuff like this,
being just like Mom is good.

We can go with the flow
and improvise anytime.

Besides, it'll be just for a few days,
because after that,
Mom will be back.

Ginny's Search

I follow Ginny through the house.
She opens every door.
And looks in every room.
and down the cellar.

She runs around the backyard.
Searches in the woods.
And looks by the clearing.

And walks right into Mrs. Evan's house
next door to search all of her rooms
and in her closets.

She searches in John's restaurant.

Ginny searches everywhere.
And I'm right here, following,
ready to rock with her
during her meltdown, because

Ginny will never find
what she's looking for.

Ginny won't find
her.

Rituals Should Never Be Broken

Norah is over for our
Friday night ritual.

She drops her bag in my room
and jumps on the bed.
"Is your mom still in Toronto recording?"

"Yeah, so we're going to have to
watch Ginny until she goes to bed."

"Can't someone else do it?" she asks.
"Looking after Ginny is boring."

"Who's going to do it?" I say.
"Ginny? Crap, Norah, you can be such a dope."

"You don't have to be so mean.
I was talking about John."

"He has to work," I say.
"There is no one else."

Norah scrunches her eyebrows.
"You've been so crabby the past few days.

No wonder your mom
left you behind."

I shove her against my bed.
"She's coming BACK!"

"That's not what I heard."
She pushes me back.

"What does that mean?" I ask,
getting right in her face.

Norah pushes me aside.
"Just things I've heard."
She yanks her bag off the floor
and stomps down the hall.
"I'm going. I don't want to be
around you anymore."

She slams the front door,
and heads down the walk,
texting on her cell.
Instead of turning right
to go home, she turns left
toward Sarah's.

I open the door and yell,
"Be that way, Norah.
I'll get a new BFF,
and you'll be stuck with
a plastic doll."

She turns around.
"Hanging out with a plastic doll
is more fun than hanging out with
boring old you."

"You'll be sorry you said that.
My mom is coming back
and we'll have lots of fun without you."

"*Whatever.*"

A Little More Smoke

The sprinkling snow
melts quickly
as it lands near the flame
of my burning stick.

I wave it,
writing my wish in the air.
Come back.

I sing, letting my voice
rise and fall
with the line of smoke,
twirling and spinning,
just like Mom did.

Pointing the stick
to the ground,
I make the smoke
wisp up around me
like the bars of a cage.
Until it floats above the trees
in rings.

A signal
Mom is sure to see,
no matter where she is.

Personality Changes

John used to have sparks
in his eyes.

He'd rush home
and sneak up on us
during slow times at the restaurant.
He'd swing us around
just to make us laugh.

And he'd laugh too,
and his laugh would be so deep,
it'd bounce off all of the

empty places

in a room.

But now that Mom's gone.
John doesn't laugh anymore.

He doesn't come home

until way past closing,
when Ginny and I are sleeping.

John comes in
drunker than Downtown Joe,
who can hardly stand without tipping.

And he makes more noise than an elephant
crashing through a circus.

So I need to get out of bed
to help him to the couch
before he wakes up Ginny

or passes out on the cold floor

and gets sick.

And when he's on the couch,
he yells at me for being awake
and tells me to go to bed.

And I think
if Mom knew
John spent all his time
working and coming home late
and drunk,
she'd come back
to take me and Ginny with her.

Sunday Morning

"Eggs."

I force my eyes open.
"Ginny."

She's standing over me. Her face
two inches from mine.
"Sunday morning. Eggs."

"Ginny, it's seven a.m.
Go back to bed.
I had a late night."

"Sunday morning. Eggs."

"Go back to bed!"

"Sunday morning. Eggs!
Sunday morning. Eggs!"
Ginny smashes her head
against mine.

"Crap, Ginny!"
I shove her away, covering

my forehead with my hand and
roll out of bed.

Ginny sits at the table,
her plate, fork, and a knife
already laid out.

"You gave me a headache.
Thanks a lot."

"You're welcome," she says.

I roll my eyes.
"When someone says
'Thanks a lot' with that tone,
you don't say 'You're welcome.'
They're being sarcastic."

"After thank you
comes you're welcome," Ginny says.

Mom taught her that.

"Not with that tone.
You need to learn to read tones," I say.

"I CAN read!
I CAN READ!"
Her forehead gets redder
every time she yells.

"Yes, you can read.
Hold this on your bump."
I press a cold cloth to her head
and look in the fridge.

"Sunday morning. Eggs."

"We have no eggs," I say.

"SUNDAY MORNING. EGGS,"
Ginny screams.

She rocks in her chair,
yelling,
"Sunday morning.
EGGS.
Monday morning.
OATMEAL.
Tuesday morning.
PANCAKES.

Wednesday morning.
BAGELS.
Thursday morning.
FRUIT.
Friday morning.
WAFFLES.
Saturday morning.
CAPTAIN CRUNCH.

"SUNDAY MORNING.
EGGS!"

Ginny is NOT
going to let this go.

I'm going to have to take her
to John's restaurant for breakfast,

   —on Early Seniors' Sunday.

"Damn it to Hell."

Seniors' Sunday at Le Bistro

Being surrounded
first thing in the morning by
fifty old people eating
a $3.99 Sunday breakfast
is about as fun as wiping out on a bicycle
and getting a bad case of road rash.

"Those yellow sneakers are horrid.
And red pants so tight
she couldn't possibly be comfortable."

"Whatever happened to proper Sunday dress?"
"I bet they're not even going to church."

"Not with that horrible black nail polish
and skull T-shirt, I hope.

"That's Satan's child through and through."

"Takes after her mother, that's for sure."

"She'll probably run from her responsibilities too."

I want to yell at those old ladies.
"I'm right here!
Do you see me running?
Maybe you should learn some manners
or at least turn up your hearing aids,
you grumpy old bags,
because everyone
in the entire restaurant
can hear your
stupid conversation."

But this is John's restaurant
and telling them straight up
would get me into trouble.
Right now, I need to do anything
not to make John mad,
so I keep it all in
and chew off my black nail polish,
waiting for Ginny to finish eating.

She's shoving her eggs in her mouth
with her fingers so fast
she's gagging.
And I'm thinking
she doesn't want to be here
any more than I do.

Keeping Up Ginny's Routine

The lady who brought the old people to Le Bistro says,
"While your Mom is away,
I hope you'll continue to bring Ginny by
to visit the seniors. Maybe you can even sing
like you used to when you were small.
We sure miss that voice of yours."

"And bring some of your dad's cookies,"
an old man says.

"I'll try," I say.
I'd rather go see Dr. Wong
and get every tooth ripped out
than bring Ginny to that place,
but it's part of her routine
so I'll do it.

Suitcase

Deep in my closet
my suitcase waits
still packed
and ready to leave.

Because before long,
depending on how Mom or John
feel about having me around,

I'll be taken back

or thrown away.

Occupational Therapy

It's Tuesday,
so it's my job to take Ginny to the clinic
on First Street for
occupational therapy.

Ginny never wants to go.
She doesn't like
interacting with people.

So even though it's just
a few blocks away,
it's a long walk
because Ginny

S T O P S

moving her feet
along the way.

And I have to tug on her jacket
to make her move again.

When we arrive
Meredith, Ginny's therapist,
is waiting.

I do my homework
while I sit in the waiting room.

By the sound of the screeching
in the other room,

you'd think Ginny was being

tortured,

but Meredith is only making
Ginny play catch.

Speaking of Torture

Sunny-Day Retirement Home
Is anything but sunny.

But Ginny just finished OT,
so her and I
stroll up to that home,

r e a l l y   s l o w,

carrying a fresh bag of John's cookies.

I'm dreading that place the whole way.
Most of those old people are grumpier
than a cornered skunk,
and they smell just as bad.

Ginny's happy to be going, though,
because she sits in their craft room
and sorts through their quilting blocks.

More than anything,
Ginny loves sorting things.
So when it's time to go,

if she's not done,
she's going to throw
a major hissy fit.
And those old people
never understand Ginny
and her fits.

They tisk and whisper,
"All that young lady needs
is a good strapping."

It doesn't matter how many times
Mom and I tell them
Ginny isn't wired like everyone else.

They don't listen

and still think they can fix her
by giving her a good whack.

And they tell me about how
when they were young,
if one of their relatives was
like Ginny and never
straightened up,

they shut them away into
special homes
or mental hospitals.

Secrets
—embarrassments

needed to be hidden
from the outside world.

Ginny is not crazy.

Even if she is embarrassing sometimes.

I'm NOT Libby

Today, after I leave Ginny to
her sorting, I go to find Mrs. Weatherall
before I sing.

She was Mom's voice coach as a child and
always loves to hear a good song,
so I want to make sure
she can hear me.

When I get to her room,
Mrs. Weatherall is slouched
in a chair beside her bed, knitting
a multicolored scarf
that would wrap around a giraffe's neck.

She looks at me,
blinks a few times,
and smiles.

"Why, Libby,
so nice of you to visit.
Have you come to sing for me?"

I shift my feet
and stare at the floor.

"I'm not Libby. I'm Casey,"
I try to explain, but
she's staring at me
like I'm an idiot
who forgot my own name.

"Libby is my mom,
remember, Mrs. Weatherall?
I'm Casey."

She stares at nothing for a bit
and gets the same distant look
Ginny gets when she's off
in her own world.

"Oh right, Casey ..."

Her voice is quiet
like she doesn't remember
but is pretending that she does,
and the smile fades off her face.
"If you're not Libby,
where is she?"

"Mom is away,
Mrs. Weatherall."

"Liar!" Mrs. Weatherall stands,
faster than I thought
an old lady could.

She smacks her cane against the tile floor,
making me drop the cookies
and jump back.

"Don't you come in here
lying to me, Libby!"
She takes a step toward me.
And smacks her cane on the floor again.

"Always getting yourself
into some kind of trouble, you are.

Pretending to be
someone else! You think
I don't know you
when I see you?"

"I am Casey. Not Libby.
I am NOT my MOTHER!"

She slams the cane again
and gets so worked up and so loud,
the nurses come flying into the room
to calm her.

But not before she can turn to me and say,
"Don't you ever come back here,
don't you ever
come back!"

I brush the tears off my face
and run, shaking, back to the craft room.

I pick up Ginny
before she has a chance
to get to the blocks that need sorting.

"Quilt blocks!"
She yells, reaching for them.

I tug her by the hand, out the door,
and down the steps, walking
toward home so quick
she has to run to keep up.

"Quilt blocks?
Quilt blocks?"
she sobs.

"Forget about the quilt blocks, Ginny.
Just forget about them," I say.
"We're not going back.
That lady doesn't know
what she's talking about.
She's just a crazy old hag."
I sniff and tug on Ginny's hand again.

"QUILT BLOCKS!"

"WE ARE NOT GOING BACK!

"No matter what Mom wants,
we're not going back, Ginny.
Not ever."

What Sign

                              if
                    the cage that
                used to trap mom
            now   traps   me   how
        big   does   my   fire
        need   to   be   so
    she'll see and   R   come back.
                          E
                            L
                              E
                                A
                                  S
                                    E

                                M E

Bad Birthdays

Ginny turned six today.
And I feel terrible
that no one but me remembered
her birthday. So I bake a cake.

I'm careful to follow the recipe
and watch it baking,
like John taught me.

And even though I know
taking time to bake
instead of doing the laundry
is going to give me
more work tomorrow,

I do it.

Because I know,
if I don't,
no one else will.
And that would be
a bad day for Ginny.
Even if she doesn't remember
it's her birthday.

Calling John

It would have taken less time
to walk to the restaurant
and ask John to come home
than to call him, because
it takes him ten minutes to
come to the phone.

"Is everything okay, Casey?"

"Yes, fine. It's just that
I made dinner.
Can you—"

"Don't let those plates go out
looking like that! Lulu,
help him fix these up!"

"John?"

"Sorry, Case,
we're right in the middle
of the dinner rush.
What did you need?"

"It's Ginny's birthday.
I made a cake.
Are you coming to sing
'Happy Birthday'?"

John doesn't answer.

"John? Are you still there?"

"Lulu, I have to leave for a few.
Keep an eye on the new guy.
Make sure he doesn't mess up."
John yells over tingling utensils.
"Be home—"
A huge crash of dishes interrupts him.
He sighs. "Be home
as soon as I can, Case."

"Okay."

"And, Case."

"Yeah, John?"

"Thanks
for making a cake."

Ginny's Fits

I wait for an hour

but John doesn't show,

so I set the cake in front of Ginny
and strike a match to

            Light the candles

poked into the top so she can

            blow them out
and make a wish,

            like a little kid should.

But Mom and John not here
changes everything

and throws Ginny into
tantrum mode.

Ginny doesn't
like

Change.

She flips the cake
across the table. It

crashes against

my juice glass.

Ginny

turns as purple
as the juice
splotch

c r e e p i n g

into the white
tablecloth.

I try to dab
the splotch

quickly

before it spreads.

But Ginny's being
a pain.

She's throwing food all
                    through
the kitchen.
She's screaming
like

                    her world
is ending.

I want to leave.

Run away
like Mom.

But if I go,
I'd be

                    tearing Ginny
                    apart.

I couldn't do that
to her.

Trying to Calm Her

I cradle her.
"It's okay. It's okay."

Rock with her.
Whisper.
Rub her back
through her shirt.

But her tears continue.

I reach to clean up a bit.

She pushes me away
and throws everything
she can reach. Until
I pull her away from the table
and drag her to her bed.

I run to my room,
curl up in the corner
behind my bed. And

cover my ears,
trying to muffle the sound of

Ginny's sobbing.

Smothering Fits

If Mom were here,
none of this would have happened.

John would have come home
and Ginny wouldn't have thrown a fit.

But now everything is
messed up for Ginny

And Mom isn't here to
help me fix it.

I have to be the one to do it,
but I can't calm Ginny
alone
as easily as Mom and I could
as a team.

I can't smother
those fits.

There's no such thing as a
team of one.

Hiding

Later, John stumbles into my room,
waking me up.

"Casey!
You better get into the kitchen
and clean up that mess."

I can't move,
my legs have fallen asleep.

He flicks on my light
and steps further into my room,
kicking one of my stuffies
across the floor.

"Casey? I don't have time
for your games."

I can smell his anger.
It smells like wine.

My heart speeds up
as he steps closer.
I could reach out and trip him,
but that would get me into more trouble,
and I can't have that.

John turns to walk away,
stops, and bends.

He reaches behind the bed
and yanks me out
by my arms.

"Now."

"I'm going!
I'm going!"

Burning Mad

I scramble off the floor
and get to the kitchen
as fast as I can.

"If I see a mess
like that in my kitchen again,
you'll be grounded for a month,"
John says as he heads for the couch.
"With your Mom away,
you're going to have to
help around the house.

"I can't do everything."

"I know. I know," I say
"I have to do it.
I'm sorry.
I was going to clean it
but fell asleep."

The cake is smooshed
into the tablecloth
and I doubt it'll ever come out.
And because it's Ginny's mess,

not mine,
I feel like Cinderella,
and wish I had some mice
to help me.

Because John's not helping.
He sits drinking his wine,
not lifting a finger to help.

And
I'm banging things in the kitchen
louder than I should.

But it doesn't matter,
because he's not
paying attention
to me.

He just sits,

      and drinks,

            sits,

                 and drinks.

When I'm done cleaning,
I curl into the covers on my bed
and wish Mom back.

Let Me Disappear

Just thinking about
the mess
I made out of the day
makes me squeeze my pillow tight
and close my eyes,
hoping to disappear into
the fire left
     Burning

inside my head.

Even More Smoke

When I hear John snoring
in the next room,
I roll out of bed
and sneak outside.

I head for the alley
behind Old Pete's restaurant,
where the garbage cans are full
of the grease-smeared newspaper
he wraps his fish and chips in.

And I light a match.

                    T

                  H E

                SMOKE of

              my fire reaches

             for the skies and

            sends my signal flying

           T O W A R D   M O M.

The Fire

It's beautiful—
blue, orange, and yellow.

Small at first,
it gets bigger
as I feed it, until
it rages,

and I feel its power
rushing through my blood,

giving me hope,

sending my signal higher,

until the sirens scream
and I know the fire
will be put out

before my signal
reaches

                       Mom.

Running into Ginny

I turn to run
but smack right into Ginny,
almost knocking her off her feet.
She just stands there in the alley,
staring at the fire behind me with
empty eyes.

"Mom says if there's a fire,
you need a drum," she says.

"Come on, Ginny."
I grab her in my arms,
to carry her home,
but she kicks my shins
and pushes me, screaming
at the top of her lungs.

"WHERE IS THE DRUM?" she says.
"Mom says!"

She throws herself back
toward the ground.

I lose my grip.
And Ginny falls,
gets up, and runs
back to the alley to
watch the fire.

The sirens are getting closer
and I try to drag her away,
but she's fighting.

The sirens are even closer
and I can't be found by a fire

I set.

Because if I am,
that'll only make things worse.

I pull her hand to come,
but she won't listen.

And Ginny keeps screaming,
"The drum.
I want to bang the drum.

Mom says at a fire
I can bang the drum."

"Sometimes Mom lies," I tell her.

Just Like My Mother

The sirens come up the street.

I HAVE to go,
because I can't be

caught,

so I leave her behind,

staring
at the flames
and whispering,

"I want to bang the drum."

Mesmerized

Hiding from the alleyway
across the street,
I watch her

I watch as the firemen find Ginny
mesmerized by the fire.

Mesmerized
by whatever she sees in her
own world.

Mesmerized
by nothing—like always.

They find her,
and she won't tell any of them
the truth,

and neither will I.

Trouble

By the time I get home,
there's a fireman
standing in the kitchen
talking to John.

I sneak in the basement window,
change into the pj's I had in the laundry,
spray my head with air freshener,
and climb upstairs,

pretending

I fell asleep
in the spare bedroom
when I couldn't sleep

in the heat

of my own room.

The Biggest Lie

"John, what's going on?"

"Casey?" John gives me
a strange look as I come up
from the basement.

I notice the fireman is John's
old friend.
"Why is Dave here—
in uniform?
Did something happen
in the restaurant?"

"They found Ginny
standing by a fire behind Old Pete's.
They don't think she set it,
but she was out there
wandering around alone."

I look at Ginny
rocking on the couch,
"How'd she get out there?
Was she sleepwalking?

She's done that before,
remember, John?
When she started school
for the first time."

John nods.
"It's the stress.
That's what we think,
but she was awake
when they found her."

"Probably confused," Dave says.
"I'm just glad I was there."

"I'll keep a closer eye on her, Dave," John says.
"I just never expected ...
Thank God you were on duty
and she didn't end up with someone else."

"I'm glad it was me too.
Had it been someone else,
she might have ended up
at the police station

while he filled out a full report."

John stares through me
like he knows
what really happened.

I look away from his eyes
and go to Ginny. Wrapping
her in my arms to make her stop rocking,
but she pushes me away.

I try again
and she screams,

so I just sit beside her, touching her hair,
wishing more than anything
she'd just look into my eyes to see

I'm sorry,

but Ginny avoids people's eyes.

And I can't get enough air
into my lungs,
knowing that because
I left her
behind,

I could have lost her.

Waiting

I sit on the edge of my bed
with my suitcase by my feet,
waiting for John to come
and say,

"Just go."

But he never does.

Locks

As soon as I wake up,
I screw a lock
on Ginny's bedroom door
so she doesn't follow me
outside at night again,
and she'll stay with us

forever.

Making Things Right

After school, I sit on a curb outside
that stupid retirement home, looking
up into those windows, thinking
about how bad I messed things up.

I sit here, looking
into those windows, thinking
if I make things good again,
I can bring Ginny back to
sort her quilt blocks
and everything will be good
and John will let me stay.

But I'm stuck staring
into those windows, trying
to make my legs move.

And as I sit here, a drop of rain
hits the top of my head,
and I look at the clouds getting
darker and darker,
and I know the higher powers are
sending me a message to get in there.

And as I sit here, looking
into those windows
I see someone wave at me from inside,
and my stomach flips,
knowing that I have
no choice now

                                    STEPS.
                          So many
                      that door.
                  toward
                steps
              those
          all

        up
      but to go

I take a breath,
swallow hard,
and climb those stairs
slow enough
that if someone saw me from
far away,
they'd think I was one of the
old ladies that live inside.

I Don't Understand Old People

I get into Mrs. Weatherall's room
and she smiles and stands up.

I stare at the floor,
step closer, and mumble,
"I'm sorry for the other day."

When she doesn't answer,
I look up.

She's watching me like
she doesn't remember
what happened.

And I know it's true.

She doesn't remember a thing,
so I let out the big breath
that I've been holding.

She smiles at me again,
and gives me a hug.

"You're a good child, Casey,
a good child,
just like your mom,
you are."

"But I'm different too,
Mrs. Weatherall," I say.
"I *am* different too."

"Of course you're different.
You're Casey.
Not Libby."

I swear,
I don't understand those old people.

Not one bit.

Annie Tryouts at School

I'm

                                    Singing,

trying out for the lead,
and when I stop,
it gets so quiet in the room
you can hear the hamster wheel
in the kindergarten class squeak.

Ms. Watts

                                    releases

her breath.

She stands to clap.

The other teachers
stand too.

And

                                    the pressures

the audition

                                    built up
                                    inside me

fly away.

And I bet Sarah
won't be whispering
anything bad
about my singing this time.

I get a standing ovation,
and with it

I beat her
for the part
of Annie.

Lulu

My insides jump so much.
I race to the restaurant to tell John.
And when I blast through the door,

John's with Lulu.

She's leaning over John,
looking at some papers
on the table in front of him.

And her being so close to him
makes me

stop

in my tracks.
Because no one should be
standing that close to John
unless it's Mom.
I push any bad thoughts
aside.

Because this is just Lulu.

And she and John have been
best friends forever.

And she's not some lady
I don't know who is
trying to steal John
when Mom's not looking.

She's Lulu, and
there's nothing going on.

So I tell them.
"I got the part of Annie!
In our end-of-the-year play!"

"Congrats, Casey!" Lulu comes
and gives me a big hug
like Mom would have.

And I don't like her being there
instead of Mom,
So I pull away.

"Great job." John's smile turns to a frown
when he looks around me and asks,
"Where's Ginny?"

I gasp. "I forgot her at school."
And my insides jump again,
not because I got the lead, but because
I left Ginny behind
for a stupid singing part.

"Well, go get her."
John taps my butt
to get me moving
and let me know
he's not mad.

But I want to kick myself
the whole way back to school.

Troublemaker

Aaron blocks
the gate to the school yard.

"Get out of my way.
I have to get Ginny."

"*I have to get Ginny?*"
Aaron sneers.

"Move," I say.

"Make me."

The grade-one teacher comes out.
Aaron moves.

"Go pick up your Freaky Sister,"
he whispers as I walk by.

"You better not be here
when I come out,
or I'll knock you one."

"You don't scare me," he says.

"Whatever," I say.

Ms. Emm waits for me
in the classroom with Ginny.
She smiles when I walk in.
"Congrats on getting the part."

"Thanks. Sorry I'm late."

"That's okay," she says.
"She just finished putting away her pencils
and is getting her jacket."

"Ginny, say good-bye
to Ms. Emm," I tell her.

"Good bye, Ms. Emm."

"See you tomorrow, Ginny," Ms. Emm says.

I grab Ginny's sleeve
and lead her out of the classroom.

When we get outside,
that chicken Aaron
is nowhere to be seen.

Getting Ready for John's Mom

When we stop at the restaurant
on the way home,
John takes me aside and whispers,
"My mother is coming to visit
for the night."

Can you clean up and
make a potpie or something?"

I nod and rush home to get to work fast.
I know it's important to John
to have everything perfect,
because in his mom's eyes
none of us can ever do
anything right.

I roll out the dough,
but Ginny throws
one of her tantrums
in the living room.

As I step over the cushions
Ginny tossed on the floor,

she chucks a book at my head.
I pull her close,
hoping to get her to stop,
and she kicks me away.

"Cut it out!" I holler.

But she screams,
"It SCRATCHES. It SCRATCHES."

"What are you talking about?"

She kicks at me again.

"Stop it, Ginny.
I don't have time for this."

I hold her foot
as she kicks one more time
and see her sock is on
with the stitching facing inward.

"Crap." I tear off her sock,
and turn it inside out before
putting it back on.

"Now the stitching isn't
touching your foot!
You could have done that
yourself.
So just stop hollering."

She stops, wipes her face
and skips away, leaving
me standing in the middle of
her mess.

"THANK YOU?" I holler
after her.

"You're welcome!"

"Ugh!"

Mom Calls

As I'm picking up
Ginny's mess,
the phone rings.

"Hello?"

"Casey!" Mom says.
"How are you?"
          "Fine.
          I beat Sarah
          for the part of Annie."

"Fabulous!
She's too prissy
for that part anyway.
How's Ginny?"
          "She's doing okay.
          I'm handling her."

"I knew you could.
You're a real lifesaver, Casey.
And John?"
          "Busy at work."

"Great. I miss you all so much."
          "When are you coming home?"
"I'm not sure.
There was a glitch
with my agent
and things have been

D E L A Y E D.

But I'm talking with a new agent,
and everything will be cleared up.
Is John home?"
          "He's at the restaurant."

"Of course he is.
I should have just called him there."

          I don't answer.
          If she'd called the restaurant
          she wouldn't have got
          to talk to me.

"Bye, Casey.
Love you."

"Love you too, Mom.
        Come home soon."

This time it's her that
doesn't answer.

Dianne Hills

I have never met anyone
as negative as
John's mom.

"You should use my recipe
for potpie next time.
Your mother isn't a good cook."

"Casey got the part of the lead
in her school play of
Annie," John says.

"Can you sing, Casey?" Dianne asks.

I sing "Tomorrow" for her.

"You sing like your mother.
        Your pitch is off too.
                You'll have to practice that,
        or you'll ruin the whole play."

"John," she says,
        "You'd get a lot more business
                in your restaurant if you served
        more French food."

"John's business is fine.
Lots of people in there
every day," I tell her.

"Casey, don't talk
        with your mouth full.
                John, are you putting
                        Ginny into a special school
                like I suggested? They'd
        help her there."

"Ginny does well
in regular school.
And her aid is fantastic
in dealing with Ginny's
special needs," John says.

"Yeah, Ms. Emm is awesome," I say,
swallowing what I have
in my mouth first.
"And Ginny goes to OT."

"Casey, I was talking to John.

                        Not you.
                        It's rude to interrupt.

            What kind of a name
        is Ms. Emm, anyway?"

I ignore her.

"Casey, you should answer
        when people talk to you."

"But you just said
you were talking to John."

"Don't talk back!
        Didn't your mother
                teach you any manners?
        Speaking of your mother,
Is she planning on
        coming back?"

"She'll come back
when she's done recording.
Right, John?" I look at him
but he's looking away.

His silence says
more
than I want it to.
And I think
Mom's chat with John
was much different
than her chat with me.
My eyes prickle,
and I fight back tears as
Dianne watches.

"I figured as much," Dianne says.

          "John, your worst mistake
                    was marrying *that* woman
                              and then taking in
                    a child that isn't even yours.

"Casey's own mother didn't *want* her.

"For Pete's sake,
get your life back and
send her to her real relatives."

I shrink in my seat,
wishing there was a hole close by
I could crawl into.

But I sit straight up
when John does
something
GREAT.

John pushes his chair
away from the table,
strolls over to his mom,
and pulls her chair back.

"The only person
I'm sending away
is you," he says.

He grabs her suitcase
from the spare bedroom
and guides her outside.
He drops her suitcase on the porch
and slams the door behind her.

"Ice cream?" he says.

"Hell, yes!"

"I beg your pardon?"

"Er ... I mean," I say,
"yes please."

How?

At school, Ms. Watts tells us
that all our practices for *Annie*
will be held in the gym after school.

And I wonder
how I can take care of Ginny,
get her to OT,
keep the house clean,
and get to the practices
all at the same time.

I wish more than anything
that I could ask for help,
but I guess I'll just have to
step things up
and go with the flow.

Worrying

I worry so much
all night long
about the trouble
Ginny will cause during my practice
that I don't sleep
and I'm grumpy
in the morning.

When I comb through her curls
and Ginny whines,
I throw the brush down and say,
"Fine! You can go to school with
a bed head."

"Bed head? I don't want a bed head!"

"A bed head is not a bed for a head.
It's just when someone has messy hair, Ginny.
It's a joke."

"You have a bed head."

"Whatever."

Obsession

"Bed Head! Mrs. Evans!"
Ginny shouts when we pass
Mrs. Evans next door.

She bends to check her hair
in the car mirror.

"Bed Head!" Ginny screams
right beside the mailman.

He jerks, dropping
the letters in his hand.
He pushes down his hat
before picking up the mail.

"Lulu, you have a bed head!" Ginny says
as we walk past her at the restaurant.

"Do I?" Lulu asks me.

I suck in my lips
so I don't laugh out loud.
"Maybe," I say.

When I glance back
she's looking into the windowpane.

Sometimes Ginny's obsessions
are hilarious.

But Sometimes They're Not

During practice Ginny flicks
the lights.

Off and on.
    Off and on.

And people trip all over the place.

The other kids and teachers get
madder and madder by the minute.

And when Ms. Watts trips
and gets up, her hair is messed.
Ginny looks at her and says,
"BED HEAD. BED HEAD."

And everyone laughs.
But I hide in the shadows.

Ms. Watts straightens her hair
and, after the red drains from her face,
she says, "Casey, is there something
we can give Ginny to
keep her occupied?

Cards or something?"

"Ginny loves puzzles.
I'll get one from Ms. Emm."

And I stomp out of the room.

Why do I have to always be
the one to do something
about my sister?

She's not *my* kid.

Pulling Ginny Home

·"Bed head!" Ginny yells at a guy
walking down his dog down the street.

"Stop it, Ginny!"
I tug her hand
to keep her moving.

"Bed head!" she says
to Mr. Evans as he rides by
on his bike.

"Ginny!
Would you just
SHUT UP
already!"

"BED HEAD!" Ginny screeches,
laughing uncontrollably,
because she thinks
you have to laugh at a joke.

When we get to our porch,
I pull her in front of me
and hold her face still
so her eyes look in mine.

"Crap, Ginny, sometimes
you make me so mad!
I wish you were never born.
If it weren't for YOU
Mom wouldn't have left me behind."

I let go of her face
and yank her into the house,
slamming the door behind us.

It's all true
—from the straight-up kid.

Nothing but the damn truth.

Regrets

Later,
while I make dinner,
Ginny sits so quiet,
lining stuffies in rows.

The light glows
around her blonde curls,
and she's looking
like some kind of angel.

And inside
it feels like stones
weighing down my heart,
and I want to just run and hug her
and make her forgive me
for wishing she weren't born.

But when I do,
she pushes me away,
because I'm bugging her.

And I smile and say,

"Love you, Ginny."

The Last Straw

After two weeks of rehearsals,
Ginny's toys are thrown
all over the house.

There's leftover chicken
on the counter
—from three days ago.

And I can't find
our bathroom floor,
because Ginny didn't like
the feel of the cold floor,
so she carpeted it in
toilet paper.

When I put a dirty shirt
on Ginny, because
I didn't get the laundry done.
She flips out,
throws stuffies
across the room and
over a row of ants tromping
through our kitchen to get to

a sticky splotch
    of spilled juice
        gelled on the floor.

That makes me scream and
            go to boot one of the stuffies
                Ginny threw,

but my sock sticks in that
    gooey pile of juice.

And I can't
    even do that right.

So I stomp to my room
    to finish my homework,

            slamming the door behind me
        and making Ginny scream,
because loud noises

hurt her ears.

And I'm so mad

I don't care.

So I slam it again.

Locking Doors

Later, John is passed out
on the couch, snoring,
with a bottle of wine
beside him.

I go check on Ginny,
because she's too quiet.
She's sleeping
and drooling on the tiles
in the middle of the kitchen floor.

I want to shove John
awake.
I want to yell at him for
walking by Ginny
without even picking her up.

But if I did that,
I couldn't send the message to Mom.

I sit Ginny up gently
and wipe off her face.

She's droopy with sleep,
so I hold her close
and rock her for a bit
before I carry her to her bed.

When I leave,
I click the lock
on her bedroom door.

Into the Fire

I take a flashlight, my *Annie* sheet music,
and Mom's djembe to
the clearing.

I strike a match and drop it into a pile
of dry leaves and sticks.

The fire warms up the coldness
stuck deep inside my belly.

I catch the edge of a flame
with the sheet music
and raise it to the sky,
watching the words

slowly

burn

away.

I grip that paper until
the flames flick my finger tips.

Let go.

And twirl beneath the music's
glowing ashes
floating on the wind
toward Mom.

I hum and twirl,
tapping lightly on the djembe,
the Burning fire by my feet,
my arms
Reaching to the sky,
Sending those words
Higher.

I twirl

       faster

faster   faster

       faster,

until I'm light inside
and my spirit is floating
up with those words.

Floating so Mom will see it.

I hum louder
        and dance nearer
                  and nearer
      to the fire's edge,
until its flames

        beg me

to dance into it.

And I'm so near,
      the flames lick my knees,
           and I lean closer,
      straight over the fire,
getting all warmed up
      inside.

The fire snaps,
      waking me
         out of my daze,
      and I jump away.

I throw dirt on it,

        smothering

                its life.

Telling Ms. Watts

Monday morning,
I wait by the classroom door
for Ms. Watts.

When she comes
I can't get my voice to work,
to tell her what I need to,
and she's standing there,
looking at me,
waiting.

And the bell rings,
and she's tapping her foot
and looking at me.
And finally she says,
"Spit it out, Casey."

And I have to swallow
hard a lot of times
before I finally say,

"I can't be Annie anymore, Ms. Watts.
I can't do it."

And my eyes are itching
to let out tears,
but I fight them back.

Swallowing really hard again,
I stare at the ground.

I turn away

and go to my seat.

I don't look at Ms. Watts
for the rest of the day.
I just stare at my desk
and don't pay attention
to her at all.

Sarah and Norah

During choir practice,
I sit in my spot
in front of Sarah and Norah,
and they're whispering
about how Sarah
is a way better Annie
than me,
and they're giggling
and saying stuff like,

"Casey's too stupid.
She couldn't memorize
all those lines anyway."

"Yeah, she can't even sing.
I bet the teachers were just
feeling sorry for her."

"Maybe she won't be here
for the play anyway."

"Do you think John
is going to send her away?"

"Maybe. She's not even his."

I throw my chorus book down,

Crush the words of Yoko Ono's
"Give Peace a Chance"
with my foot

as I
Push past Norah and Sarah
and
Stomp out of the room
before I
Bust both of their faces
right there in front of Ms. Watts.

Retreat

In a perfect world Mom would be here.
In a perfect world I wouldn't miss her.
In a perfect world my days would be
N   O   R   M   A   L
A   N   D   **GINNY**   T   O   O
N   O   T   L   O   S   T
in her own world. In a perfect world I'd
spend my days doing normal kid stuff.
In a perfect world I would not want to
retreat into my head the way Ginny does.

A Perfect Kind of Tantrum

During recess, Ginny and I are trying to
mind our own business,
but Norah and Sarah are practicing
right in front of us.

Every so often they look our way,
grin, and really put on the acting
so it's so fake
but so loud they know I can hear.

Then Sarah messes up
big time,
missing a bunch of lines
before going into the song
"I Think I'm Gonna Like It Here."

Norah glances up at me quickly.
I know her expressions. She's hoping
I didn't notice
Sarah missed a whole lot of lines
between the word *windows* and the song.

I sneer at her,
because Norah knows
my expressions and realizes

I did notice.

While I'm sneering
a wasp lands on Ginny's red jelly cup,
and she freaks out and chucks it,
waving her arms at the wasp
until it flies away
and I calm her down.

But when I look up,
Sarah is glaring at us
and picking red jelly
out of her long blonde hair.

And I grin at her. "I guess now
you have the red hair you need
to play the part of Annie."

"You did that on purpose,"
Sarah says.

"Whatever. Ginny threw it.
Norah knows
Ginny can't help it.
I can't change the fact that
she's autistic.
If I could change things,
that would be second on my list."

"What would be first?" Sarah says.
"Your face?"

"No, your memory.
You just messed up your lines
big time," I say.

"Whatever."
She turns away,
dragging Norah behind.

"Good shot, Ginny.
Good shot," I say.

"Sticky."

Ginny's coat is thrown on the steps
and she's pulling at her shirt.
"Clothes stay on
in the school yard!"

I carry her to the girls' change room,
praying to get inside fast enough
she doesn't have time
to take her shirt off.

Tuesday OT

Meredith takes us both
for a walk in the park.

She tells me,
"Ginny is acting out
through more fits at home,
because she knows she feels
bad. But she doesn't understand why."

"She keeps looking for Mom," I say.

"She will for a while.
But the longer your mom is away
the more likely Ginny will reach a point
where she doesn't know who she's looking for.
She'll just know there's
someone missing."

I watch Ginny twirling
on the swing.

She blurs
in the tears
I'm fighting to hold back.

Sunny-Day

"Quilt blocks?" Ginny asks.

Why couldn't Ginny
forget about Sunny-Day
the way Meredith said
she'll forget Mom?

"Yes. We can go."

After stopping at the restaurant
to pick up cookies,
we head over to Sunny-Day.

Mrs. Weatherall is in the common room
and at first I don't want to stick around,
but right away she says,
"Casey, are you going to sing?"

"Umm ... okay."
I pick up a guitar in the corner
and sit down to sing one of
Mom's favorite songs,
"Me and Bobby McGee."

As I'm singing
Ginny is sorting.

"Old age has got me losing
my memory," Mrs. Weatherall says.

And her mind.

"Which color comes next?"
Before she can figure it out,
Ginny is standing in front of her,
holding a floral printed triangle.
Mrs. Weatherall smiles.
"That was speedy, Ginny dear.
Good job.
Can you hand me the next?"

Ginny does.

On the table, Ginny
lines up a whole row of triangles
for Mrs. Weatherall's pattern.

I come to the end of the song
and pay no attention to the clapping.

Instead I watch as
Ginny lines up another row.

The other quilters watch,
mouths open.
They whisper to each other.

"Why, that child is brilliant."
        "Amazing, how she figured that out so fast."
"That's not an easy pattern Lonnie is sewing."
      "Not at all. It's complicated—very complicated."
 "And the girl did it. All by herself."

    "That little girl is as smart as a whip."

I grin at Mrs. Weatherall,
and she winks
and whispers to me,
"I was tired of them saying
Ginny needed to be
in a home."

I hug her.
 "Thank you."

I'd come visit Mrs. Weatherall
anytime,
even if she does
think I'm Mom.

Thinking Outside the Box

We head to the restaurant to celebrate
Ginny's breakthrough
with the old ladies.

John serves us each
a bowl of ice cream.
Cherry.

"Ginny only likes vanilla, John," I say.

"We're unloading the truck.
It's way in the back."

"Vanilla," Ginny says.

"This is vanilla, Ginny,
with cherries," I tell her.

"Vanilla."

"Think outside the box."

"I'm not in a box," she says.

"Thinking outside the box
means to do something
different.
Just try it," I say.

Ginny takes a spoonful.

"Sweet.
Chewy.
Creamy.
Cold."
She keeps eating.

"She likes it?" John asks,
sitting beside me.

"Guess so. She
hasn't stopped eating."

"I'll be working late again, Casey.
Otherwise, I don't know how I'll get done
what needs to be done," John says.

Ginny stops eating.
"Think outside the box.
Means to do something different."

Perfect timing.

Aaron

During lunch, I sit alone
on the step outside our school
and watch Ginny playing by herself
by the swings.

Aaron Taylor struts up
and hands her Play-Doh.
"It's just like gum."

"Thank you—When someone
gives you something. You say thank you,"
Ginny says as she pops it into her mouth.

I'm glued to the step,
hoping the teacher will stop it,
because I know
if I go,
I'll hit him,
and that will get
me into trouble,
and Mom isn't here
to stand up for me.

He laughs when she spits it out.

"Freak,

        freak,"

he says.

Ginny whimpers.
She throws herself on her back,
kicking and banging her hands
against the ground.

Ginny is

        Screaming.

                And Kicking.

                        And Punching sand.

And Aaron laughs.

"You're a freak.

        Freak.

                Freak.

                        Freak."

I wait,
but the teacher is busy
breaking up a fight
on the other side of the playground
and Aaron hasn't touched her.

But no one else is stepping in,
except Aaron's friends, who see
the teacher busy,
so they come and kick sand at
my little sister.
Just to watch her flip out more.

And there's no
stopping
any of it.

And my nails are digging
so hard
into my palms,
I bleed.

And my teeth are
grinding together so tight,
I'm giving myself
a headache as I sit back
and watch,
and see
no one
stopping it.

Stepping In

By the time I get there,
Ginny is covered in sand
and tears pour from her eyes,
pushing out grains of sand
with them.

And the boys are too busy kicking
and chanting to notice me.

I grab Aaron by the shoulders
and flip him on his back.
He hits the ground with a thud,
and I jump on top of him.

"Leave Ginny alone!" I scream,
thumping my fists against his head.
"Leave her alone, you creep!"

Blood spurts out of his nose,
and he covers his face with his hands.

His friends tear me off him
and dump me on the ground
beside Ginny.

Aaron stands up and scoffs,
"You fight like a wuss."
He wipes his fist
against his bloody nose.
"You're going to be in trouble
when I tell Ms. Watts.
Everyone's waiting for John to dump you—you know?
And picking you up
in the office for fighting
will give a him a good reason."

I shove Aaron.
"I didn't start this
and you know it. And I bet
your dad isn't going to be
pleased to hear about you
kicking sand
at a little kid, either."

Aaron shrugs like
he doesn't care what his dad does,
but I can tell
by the way his smile falls,
he won't be telling Ms. Watts
the truth about how he got that
bloody nose.

Brushing Sand

I think about Aaron and his friends
as I brush the sand piles off Ginny
and wash her eyes out
in the girls' bathroom.

"I'll get him for this," I whisper.
"I'll get him and
he'll be sorry."

I shake the sand off Ginny's head
a little too rough,
and she whimpers,
"Too hard."

"Sorry."

I take Ginny back to her classroom early.

"She got sand in her face," I say to Ms. Emm.
"But she's fine now.
She just doesn't want
to be outside anymore."

Ms. Emm nods
and I take off for home.

The Bike

I'm late getting back to school, and
as kids are going inside,
this side of
the playground is as still
as a Sunday morning
before the old folks come
to Le Bistro for breakfast.

I squirt the lighter fluid

I took from Mrs. Evan's garage

and strike a match.

The fire poofs
like a banana flambé.

And I race back to class
with the stench of burning rubber
filling my nose.

Sirens

... stir up our class
during English
as we rush
to the windows.

A bike sits
in the bike stand,
parked by the owner

far from the others,
so it doesn't get scratched.

The decals on its frame
crackle and shrivel up in chunks.

Black smoke hovers over the seat
as it melts and drips
like candles.

And Aaron Taylor wails,
"That's my bike!"

Heads High

On the way home,
I hold my head high
as Ginny and I stroll past
the blackened bicycle
hand in hand.

I shouldn't have gone
that far.

It was wrong.

I know it.

But no one messes
with my little sister.

Lulu

When we get home,
Lulu
is sitting in the kitchen drinking tea
with John.

"Hi, girls," she waves.
"How are you today?"

"I'm good," I say.

"Fine," Ginny says. "When someone
asks how you are.
You say fine."

John smiles.
"I don't need you
to watch Ginny today, Case,
if you want to go out and play
with your friends."

I blink at him
for long enough to make
Lulu shift in her seat

and look into her glass,
like she's reading her fortune
in her tea leaves.

"Who's looking after the restaurant?"

"Donald."

"The new guy?"

"Yeah, he turned into quite the worker.
We're testing him out. See how well he does
unsupervised."

So I shrug and say,
"Okay."

But my stomach knots up
when I realize,
I don't have friends left
to play with.

Help

Lulu and John start talking
about me quitting the play
because I wanted to stay home
and look after Ginny
and help around the house.

And Lulu says,
"That's just terrible, Casey.
You need to have fun
and be a kid."

"No I don't.
Ginny needs me."

"Sure you do.
I wish you didn't have to quit
because of that."

She turns and looks at John.

"You know, with Donald at the restaurant,
I could come over here
and look after Ginny
so Casey can get to those rehearsals."

My head's spinning.
I want to be Annie so bad.
But I've got responsibilities
and I can't just dump them all
for a singing gig,
no matter what.

Another change
isn't fair for Ginny.

John makes up my mind for me
and says, "I think that's a great idea.
Between Lulu, me, and Donald,
we can handle this."

And he turns to me and winks.
"Now you can show Sarah
how Annie is supposed to be played."

I blink like an idiot again
before I race over to him
and hug him tight enough,
I can make myself know
it's all for real.

John picks me up in his arms
and spins me around,
like he used to.
And inside, my heart
is filled up
again.

But if Lulu learns to handle Ginny,
what will John need me for?

Understudies

Because I want my part back,
that stupid Sarah is throwing a bigger fit
than Ginny when someone tries to hug her,
and I don't like it.

Not one little bit.

"You can't let her take it, Ms. Watts,"
Sarah says, glaring at me.
"Casey hasn't been here
for all the rehearsals like me."
She stomps her foot.
"It's not going be fair
if she gets it back,
because I've worked so hard
at playing Annie."

Ms. Watts turns to me,
"I'm afraid Sarah is right, Casey.
You've missed too many rehearsals,
and she's been working awfully hard.
I just can't give you the part back."

I slouch in my seat
and stare at my desk.

"I tell you what, though," Ms. Watts says.
"If you come to every rehearsal,
you can be Sarah's understudy."

Understudy sounds like Sarah would be
teaching me something,
and I doubt I could handle
being taught anything
by Sarah Cunningham.

When I don't answer,
Ms. Watts asks,
"Do you know what
an understudy is?"

I shake my head.

"It means you'll take over the part
if Sarah gets sick and can't play it."

"I guess that will be okay."
I glance at Sarah,
hoping she ends up with the itchy chickenpox
Ginny and I had two years ago,
because leaving Ginny
for someone else to take care of
is even worse
just to be someone's understudy.

Best Child

John doesn't like
the fact that I lost the part
because he was late
thinking up a solution.
I can tell by the way the
corners of his mouth drop
when I tell him and Lulu.
He shakes his head slowly
and looks at the floor.

But Lulu says,
"I'm so sorry, Casey.
I wish we could have thought of
this arrangement sooner."
She hugs me close.
"But I'll still help
and you go to rehearse anyway."

And John smiles
like he used to.
"I guess we'll just have to hope
Sarah Cunningham loses her voice.
So the best child
can sing the part."

Not Mom

Seeing Lulu cooking
in Mom's kitchen
makes my stomach
flip-flop.

I like

the freedom,

but seeing her in Mom's place
when I should be there
is like being hit by a back draft
that throws me totally off course.

Sick

Because Ms. Watts is sick,
I don't have practice today,
and on the way home,
Aaron creeps up closer and closer
to me and Ginny.

"Freaks, freaks, freaks," he chants
as we walk.

"Leave us alone, Aaron." I move faster,
pulling Ginny by the hand
so she's almost running.

Aaron speeds up too.
He reaches out and
yanks Ginny,
jerking her back.

She falls.

I lean to help her up,
but Aaron shoves me to the ground
and pins me down.

He bends close to my ear and says,
"You and your little freaky sister
aren't good for nothing.
No wonder your mom took off."

He reaches over
and smacks Ginny's face.

And I snap.

Kicking Butt

If there's anything I learned how to do
when I was on the road with Mom,
it's fighting dirty. I've seen more fights
than a nightclub bouncer.

Fighting is like riding a bicycle.
Those things,
you never forget.

So as Aaron's hand leaves
Ginny's face,
my fist is heading straight
for his nose.

Before he can react,
I give him a knee to the groin,
and as he's bent over,
it's an uppercut to the chin.

If Aaron Taylor
knows what's best for him,
he won't want to bug
Ginny or me
ever again.

"Did you see him run, Ginny?"
I ask, as we skip home.
"Did you see that?
He ran away like a pansy boy."

Ginny looks straight ahead.
"Aaron has a bed head."

I grin,
pick her up,
and swing her around.
"Come on,
This deserves ice cream."

Good Times

When we're sitting,
eating our ice cream,
John comes in humming.

He grins at us,
picks me up,
and spins me around
like I had just done to Ginny,
except I don't scream
like she did.

He sees the ice cream drips
I left on the counter
and stops in midspin.
He stares at it for a while,
and I'm getting jumpy inside
because he doesn't like messes
in the kitchen.

And his jaw bulges at the sides,
like when he's mad.

But he turns to me and says,
"Hummm, the splotches
are kind of shaped like a dog."

I look and he's right.
I see a dog too.

He wipes it off and
gets himself a bowlful.
And we all sit there
together,
eating just ice cream
for dinner.

Too Quiet

Things are too quiet
                        in the house.

I put away the dish
I'm drying,

And check on Ginny.
                        I find her

standing in my room,
holding a
                        burning
match below
                        her palm.

                        She doesn't feel it.

I turn her palm over
and see a red spot.

                        My heart jumps
                        into my chest so fast
                        I throw up.

Sending Lulu Home

Ms. Watts is still sick today,
so I bring Ginny home.

Lulu is looking
way too comfortable
chopping veggies
in Mom's kitchen.
Walking around
like she owns the place.
If Lulu comes in
and Mom doesn't have
a place here anymore,
where will that leave me?

When Lulu pulls out
John's favorite cookie recipe
I think about that saying,
"The way to a man's heart
is through his stomach,"
and I've had enough.

"You can go now.
I can do it," I tell her.

"It's okay, Case," she says.
"I got it. Why don't you
do your homework
and practice your lines."

"You're not my mother.
Don't tell me what to do."

As she turns to look at me,
the color creeps slowly
into her face.
"Casey? Are you okay?"

"Fine. I said I can do it
and I'll do it. I don't need
anyone's help.
So you can go
back to the restaurant."

"I didn't say—"

"How's my girl?"
John comes in from outside
and hugs me.

"Just about to finish making dinner.
You going to be here?"

"I have to get back,
but I won't be home late."
He looks around.
"You're turning into
quite the cook, Case.
Keep it up and
we'll have you
working in the restaurant
before you know it.
Won't we, Lulu?"

"Yup," Lulu says,
looking away from him.

"See you later, Lulu," I say,
hugging John closer.

Lulu leaves for the restaurant,
letting the screen door
slam behind her.

Calming Ginny

Ginny throws a fit
in her room.

And John's in there
trying to calm her,
but she keeps screaming.

I know I'm going to have to go,

but I wait,
and keep studying the lines.

He needs to learn how to do it
without me.

"Casey!" he yells.

I put my book down
and hurry to Ginny's room.

John holds her on the bed,
trying to get her arms
through a pj top.

But Ginny shoves him away,
kicking and banging
the back of her head
against the wall.

She's been screaming so bad,
her face is turning purple.

John says,
"Handle it, please?
I can't do it.
She won't let me."

He lets her go, frustrated,
and brushes past me,
leaving the room so fast
I feel a breeze.

"Crap, Ginny.
Why can't you just let him do it?
Everything is going good.
Don't mess it up."

She's still screaming
as she chucks the pj top
across the room.

I should have just given those pj's away.

Ginny doesn't like
the cold of satin.

She stares at her wall
and rocks on her bed.

I let her rock
until her face turns her normal color.

I grab her flannel pj's.
"I'm coming, Ginny."
I stretch her arms high,
and tickle her armpits,

just like Mom used to do with me,
but Ginny screams,

so I stop.

"Sorry, Gin." I lift her arms again
and slide them into her shirt.
"That's better than those
stupid satin pj's, eh, Ginny?"

She bends over and rests her forehead
against the cold headboard.

I sit beside her
and sing one of the songs
Mom used to sing to me.

I get so wrapped up in the word
and the way my heart is beating
because of that song,
for a long time,
I don't notice,
that she's staring
at me.

And the shock of seeing her eyes
looking into mine
makes mine tear.

Being the Same but Different

Now that Ginny is calm

I stand and do one of my "whacky dances"
until she starts laughing again.

Mom says it's our little quirks,
like dancing with no music
and hiding our real feelings
with laughter,
that make us the same.

But the fact that
I'm standing here
beside Ginny.

And she's not.

Makes us different
and that gives me hope.

Awful Day

It's a horrible practice after school.
Sarah whispers to Norah again,
and laughs.
And I haven't done anything
to deserve it.

But Sarah whispers anyway.
And this time it's not about me.

It's about Ginny.

And Ginny hasn't done anything to her, either.
And Sarah says Ginny's stupid

when it's not even true.

And they laugh about her,
        and make fun of her,
                and mimic her fits,
                        right in front of me.

                Norah's got some nerve
        laughing with Sarah as

Sarah flaps her hands

and makes humming noises.

And even though Norah

avoids looking at me,

she doesn't stick up for Ginny

when she knows

Sarah is full of crap.

She doesn't

stick up for Ginny

when she's been

to my house,

and played with

Ginny and me,

and eaten

our cookies,

and been to

our birthday parties,

and been my

best friend forever.

She does not

stick up for

Ginny.

And all
    my anger
        is burning
            inside of me
                and it's getting
                    so hot

                    I punch Norah
               right in the mouth,
                  because she
                 didn't stick up
             for my little sister
            when she knows
              what Sarah said
                  isn't true.

Grounded

John is so mad about being pulled
from work when the principal calls him
and tells him to come get me
for fighting.

"Casey, WHAT has got into you?
Fighting?
With Norah?
Isn't she your best friend?"

"She was.
But now she's
mean," I say.

"It doesn't matter.
You shouldn't have hit her."

"But they were—"

"No hitting!
Get to your room
and do your homework.
I don't want to hear
another peep about it.

You're *grounded*."

"But—"

"ROOM—NOW.
I'm going back to work.
Don't leave that room."

"Fine! I'm going!" I yell,
banging my way up the stairs.
"But Mom wouldn't have taken
their crap! If someone did to her
what Norah did to me and Ginny,
Mom would have knocked
that person clear to Quebec!
No doubt about it!"

"Your mother is not here," John says.

"I can FREAKING see that, damn it!"

Mom Would Have Listened Too

Give me a chance
            to say what
I need to say
        WHY

I can't keep doing this

                LISTEN to ME

        SCREAMING
                    DON'T
Turn away

        I NEED YOU

BE HERE

        HELP ME, PLEASE

                READ MY SIGNALS

        I'm disappearing

I'm going up in

        FLAMES

Stupid Suitcase

That stupid suitcase
is out of the closet again,

waiting.

But John's too busy
at the restaurant
to come home
and send me away.

I guess *that's* something
to be thankful for.

No More Annie

Just because I punched
Norah
in the mouth,
I'm not allowed
to even be the understudy
for that stupid Sarah,
when it was all her fault
in the first place.

Pushing Lulu Away

Lulu brings Ginny
home from school
and makes dinner.

We sit around the table
eating our chicken,
not hardly saying anything at all.

"If you need to talk to someone
about something, Casey,
you know you can talk to me."

"I'm fine.
We're fine.
We don't need you.
If I need to say anything
I can say it when Mom gets back."

I don't like the pity expression
on Lulu's face.

I don't like it at all.

It makes me so nervous,
I don't pay attention
and accidentally
scrape my fork across the plate,
making a high-pitched noise.

Ginny screams
and covers her ears.

Lulu jumps
and tries to calm Ginny.
But her fussing
makes things worse.

Ginny would have stopped without it.
But now, Ginny's kicking and screaming,
and pushing her away.

And Lulu tries
harder,
but Ginny doesn't like
being touched.

Not at all.

And I could help Lulu,

because I know
Ginny will calm down

if Lulu
stops
touching her,
because the scraping noise
is gone.

but even though I like Lulu

okay,

I like watching her
fail miserably

more.

Because if she fails,
there's no chance
she'll try to take Mom's place
in our house.

Ginny throws a full-blown tantrum,
banging her head on the table and
into her mashed potatoes,
spraying them and the gravy
all over Lulu.

And starts freaking out more
because she's dirty.

And Lulu backs away,
shaking her head and crying.

"I can't do it.
I can't. I don't know how
to handle Ginny.
I'm sorry."

"That's fine.
No one asked you to.
I can handle Ginny myself."

I lift Ginny out of her chair
as she kicks and screams.
She tears my face with her nails,
all the way to her room.

I put her on her bed
and sing to her
to calm her down.

When Ginny's calm
I go back to the kitchen.

Lulu is gone.

Lost

I thought that if

        I drove Lulu
        away,

things would be

        the way
        Mom would want

them to be
and I'd feel better.

        Now

that she's gone,

        I feel lost.

Last to Know

Norah and Sarah snicker
as Ginny and I walk by.

"We saw your mom's pic
on the Internet last night,"
Sarah says.

"Yeah, at a big party
in LA," Norah says.
"Bet you didn't even know
she was out of Toronto,
let alone out of Canada."

"Of course I knew," I say.
"Her new agent's in LA.
She phones all the time."

I pull Ginny past them.

Mom's in LA?
No wonder she can't see
my signals.

fire

I doesn't matter
how big a fire
I build.

Mom never sees the signals.

How can she
from California?

But I have to keep trying.

I need her to see them
more than ever.

Because right now
I just want to lie down
and fall asleep
inside the fire
I built.

She MUST Have Seen

**T
he
ph
one
rings**

* *

\# \# **DON HINKEY AGENCY** \# \#

* *

But when I answer, it's Mom and I
think she's calling to say she saw
my signal and is coming right home
But instead she says, "I won't be
home anytime soon." Her life is
CRAZY. She doesn't have time to ask
about us." The only words spilling
from her super-famous lips are: *my
deal, my contract, my agent, my movie,
my world tour, my fans*. This stupid
call's all about Mom's new life without
me. I say, "I have to go now, I guess
if I want to get in touch with you, all
I need to do is dial up your **megastar
Libby # IDO-NOT-CARE.**"   click

Skipping

Today during lunch recess,
instead of going to choir practice,
because I can't stand

to be around Sarah and Norah,

I go into the back woods
and build another fire.

I beat hard on the djembe
and dance and chant and swirl.
But no matter what I do,
I know Mom
is never going to see
my smoke signals
and come back for me.

She
doesn't
want
to.

The Fight

On the way home,
Aaron creeps up on us again,
but this time it's with his friends.

They chase me and Ginny into the alley.

And two of them beat on me
while the others push Ginny

back
      and
            forth
      back
and
      forth
            between them.

When she stumbles and falls,
scraping her knees
and forehead on the cement,
Aaron kicks her.
And it takes all three of his friends
to hold me down,

so Aaron can get away.

Carrying Ginny

I stumble toward home,
holding Ginny really close
as she cries.

Her weight is
pulling
at my arms.

They ache

along with my insides.

And I whisper,
"I'll get you home.
I'll get you there.
I can take care of you, Ginny,
I can.

       Just like Mom wants.
       I can.
       And I won't let
       anyone hurt you
       ever again."

Blame

John races out of the restaurant
and follows us home
when he sees us coming.

"What happened?"

                          John

looks at us, all
scratched up
and bleeding.

"What happened, Casey?"

He looks at me like he

                          Blames

me. Like I hurt my own sister.

His face is turning red,
and he's glaring at

                          Me

Like I did it.

He's coming at me

LIKE I DID IT!

"You've been fighting,
and Ginny is hurt
because of it!"

He yells.

"Casey, why were
you fighting?"

I pull Ginny closer.
I step away
from him, bring her
into the house.
"I can take care of her!"

He pulls Ginny

from my arms
and places her in a chair
and checks her over.

He Blames me.

And turns on me.

"Casey, *what*
did *you* do?"

"But I didn't—"

He reaches for me
and shakes me hard.

"What did you *do*?"

        "John ... please ...
                                    I didn't do it,
        it was Aaron Taylor."

"You were fighting
Aaron Taylor?"
He shakes me again.
"You were fighting *him*?"

                                    I try to tell him,
                                    I didn't do it.

                                    I try to tell him

what happened,

                                    but my head is
                                    shaking.

I try to tell him,
but my brain is
exploding.

I try to tell him,
but I can't get
the words out.

I try to tell John but,

                   he doesn't hear me,

he's shaking me up
so hard

                   the fire inside me
                   BURNS
                   too hot.

He's shaking me up
so much

                   I'm going to
                   EXPLODE.

Running Away

I push away from him
and run out of the kitchen
and into the woods.

I run
until my heart
pumps so fast,
it's bursting through my chest.

I run
away from John,
away from Ginny,
away from my responsibilities.

I keep running.

Away.

And only when I think
I'm far enough away
from John
and his stupid restaurant
do I stop and collapse on a log and cry.

The Search

They're looking for me.
I can hear their calls
through the fog,
through the cold,
through the night.
All through the woods
I hear their calls.

I hear John.
And Lulu.
And Norah
and her dad
and her mom.

I hear everyone
calling desperately
in the woods
for me.
But I'm not lost.

I'm home,
sifting through the back of my desk,
looking for that letter.

I HATE Envelopes

Envelopes let words play hide-and-seek.

Words like:

"Sorry"

and "This is best for everyone"

and "I'll die here"

and "I love you."

I don't have to open
the damn envelope to know
what words are hiding inside.

Because the number one thing I hate most
about envelopes is that

Envelopes let the word

"Good-bye"

win the game.

Every

single

time.

Mom Isn't Coming Back

I know, because

Ginny is the door to Mom's cage

and I am the key.

A Sack Full of Memories

I rush around
the silent house
with a pillowcase,
tossing in anything
I see that reminds
me of my mom.

Burning Traces of Mom

Gripping John's minitorch
in my sweaty palm,
I throw a stack of newspapers
into the dumpster behind Le Bistro
and pour a bottle of brandy over top.

Then flick the switch.

It poofs.

The fire travels up the
        back of the dumpster.

And I tear apart Mom's sheet music,
        and song lyrics.
                I chuck their pages into the fire.
        I throw in her CDs
        and childhood pictures,
the ones that look

                just like me.

I throw in her djembe,
her guitar picks,
her gold records,
and her Grammy.
I throw in the envelope
hiding Mom's good-bye
words to me.

I toss in another brandy bottle.
It smashes in the heat.
And the fire grows bigger.

It reaches past the top
of the dumpster and crackles
the paint on the restaurant wall,
and its flames crawl up
the side of Le Bistro
and seep into the open window.

I slam the dumpster closed,
            burning my hands,
        and run inside to douse the fire
that snuck inside.
But it's already running along
            a line of cooking oil
                someone has spilled
                    on the floor.

And the alarms are screaming.
And the sprinklers turn on inside.

But water won't put out
        an oil fire in the kitchen.
That fire grows.

I turn to run
but trip over a chair,
and fall.

Through the cloud of smoke,
 I see the corner of a table
  coming straight at my face.
 And everything
around me is
 swallowed up
 by black.

John

I wake, coughing.
My chest burns with
breaths of hot air.

Someone carries me

out of the heat.

Before the darkness
fills my head again,

I look up
and see
John.

Sirens

I hear
Sirens.
And voices.
But mostly Sirens.
They sound like
they are coming
from inside my
floating head.

Lucky

I overhear doctors saying
I'm lucky.
Other than my hand,
I'm not burned,
but inside me
everything
is so
hot.

Kiss

John is sitting beside my bed,
brushing the hair away from my face
like Mom used to when I was sick.

I don't open my eyes,
but I feel the wetness
on his face
when he bends
and kisses mine.

Avoiding Good-byes

I don't want to wake up
and face the music.

Because everyone will know
that I set all of those other fires.

They'll know that I left Ginny.

They'll know about the bike.

And John will be so mad,
I'm certain he'll have
my suitcase
waiting on the doorstep
in the same spot
he put his mother's.

And I'll have to say good-bye
to my life here.
Good-bye to John
and Ginny.

I want to just stay in the hospital
and run away from all the good-byes,
just like
my mother
ran away
from all of us.

Sorry

When I get home,
my suitcase is on the porch.

The rock hard inside me crumbles
into a pile of rubble,

and I sink on the step
in front of John.

"Sorry for setting fire to Le Bistro,
but PLEASE let me stay.
Please, John,
I'll be good.
I'll look after Ginny.
I won't sing anymore.
PLEASE don't send me away."

John pulls me up off the step,
hugs me hard,
and taps my suitcase
with his foot,

so I can see it's
... open and empty.

John's Sorry

John wraps me
in his arms and whispers,
a whole lot of sorry.

"Sorry. I didn't mean to
make you think
I was kicking you out.
The suitcase was on the step
to let you know
you're not going anywhere.

And neither am I."

A Family Meeting

Lulu is in the kitchen
doing a puzzle with Ginny.

"Casey!"
Lulu jumps from her chair
and hugs me.
"I'm so glad you're okay.
You had us all scared there
for a while."

I hide my face in her arms,
not wanting her to let go.

"Come sit down," John says.
"There's something we need to
talk about as a family."

I'm expecting an
earful of trouble
from John.

But Lulu winks,
and as I let out the breath
I was holding,
John breathes one in.

He glances at Lulu.

She nods,
urging him on.

"Casey, I'm not your
real dad," he says.

I bite my lip
and look down.

"But I'd like to be," he says.

I gasp,
snapping my head up
to look at him.
My dad?

"I want to legally
adopt you." He lets the words
spill from his lips like
he's nervous.
"Your mom likes the idea.
If you like it?"

LIKE it?

John shifts in his chair
and I look from him to Lulu,
hoping she'd nod
and let me know
his words are real.

"It doesn't mean your mom
won't be your mom
anymore," Lulu says.
"No matter what happens
nothing is going to change that.
It just means John will be
your dad."

I swallow the guilt
building in my throat
for treating her so bad,
because she's always here
when we need support.

John says, "You don't have to
answer this minute. You can
think about it."

"Okay," I say.

"Okay, you'll think about it?" he asks.

When he moves his chair,
it squeaks against the floor
and Ginny screeches.
Lulu reaches for her,
and I reach for Lulu,
holding her back
just long enough.
Ginny stops.

"No," I say.

"I mean, okay,
Dad."

John jumps from his chair
and hugs me,
and I feel safe knowing this:
No matter where Mom is,
Dad will never leave me.

He is mine,
and I am his,
both of us settlers.